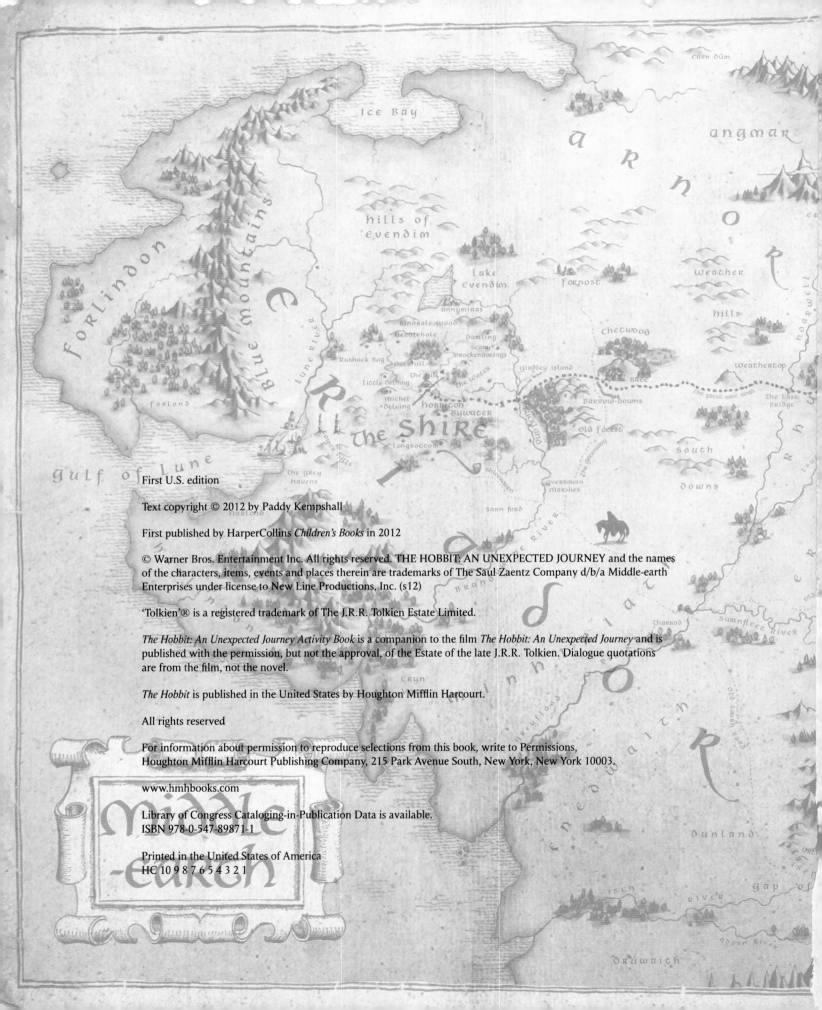

First U.S. edition

Text copyright © 2012 by Paddy Kempshall

First published by HarperCollins *Children's Books* in 2012

The Hobbit: An Unexpected Journey Activity Book is a companion to the film *The Hobbit: An Unexpected Journey* and is
published with the permission, but not the approval, of the Estate of the late J.R.R. Tolkien. Dialogue quotations
are from the film, not the novel.

The Hobbit is published in the United States by Houghton Mifflin Harcourt.

For information about permission to reproduce selections from this book, write to Permissions,
Houghton Mifflin Harcourt Publishing Company, 215 Park Avenue South, New York, New York 10003.

www.hmhbooks.com

Library of Congress Cataloging-in-Publication Data is available.
ISBN 978-0-547-89871-1

Printed in the United States of America
HC 10 9 8 7 6 5 4 3 2 1

THE HOBBIT™

AN UNEXPECTED JOURNEY

Activity Book

Houghton Mifflin Harcourt

Boston   New York

CONTENTS

Bilbo Baggins

Like all hobbits, Bilbo is fond of his comfortable life in the Shire. However, when the Wizard, Gandalf, and 13 Dwarves unexpectedly appear on his doorstep, his Tookish spirit of adventure gets the better of his Baggins good sense and changes his life forever.

Bilbo likes to keep a journal, and his adventures with the Company of Dwarves mean he certainly has a lot to write about!

Bilbo's home is a very fine hobbit hole called Bag End. With a full larder and a cheery fire, it's as warm and cosy a place as you could imagine.

Good hobbits always have something tasty cooking in the oven. Bilbo was certainly glad he had lots of food in the house when Thorin and his 12 hungry companions appeared one afternoon and decided to stay for dinner!

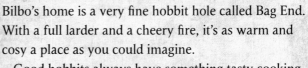

When Bilbo agrees to join Thorin Oakenshield, little does he know that a plain gold ring he finds along the way will be more precious than all of the treasure in the whole of Middle-earth.

On his adventures, Bilbo finds Sting – an Elven weapon made in the ancient city of Gondolin. It was used in the great Goblin wars and glows blue whenever Orcs and Goblins are near!

Bilbo is perhaps the most unexpected choice to join a band of heroes on a quest to steal a dragon's treasure, but along the way it is his bravery and skill that save everyone from disaster time and time again.

DID YOU KNOW?

Hobbits' large, hairy feet are so tough they can walk anywhere without wearing shoes or socks!

PANTRY PUZZLE

Look closely and see if you can spot the 8 differences
between these two pictures of Bilbo and his visitors.

A.

B.

COMPANY CONTRACT

Thorin has heard of your deeds and wants you to join the Quest for the Lonely Mountain, just like Bilbo! If you think you have the skills, sign the contract as Burglar and begin your adventure.

In role as **Burglar** for Thorin and Company, or in any other role they see fit, at their sole discretion from time to time.

Signed: *Thorin son of Thrain*

Witnessed: *Balin son of Fundin*

Burglar:

THE UNEXPECTED JOURNEY

When Bilbo agreed to join Thorin Oakenshield on his Quest to the Lonely Mountain, he had no idea of the adventures ahead of him. Follow the Company's path on this map and see where Bilbo's travels will take him.

RIVENDELL

The Elf-Haven of Imladris. A magical valley which is the home of Elrond and the Last Homely House East of the Sea. Hidden amongst the shadows of the Misty Mountains, Rivendell is a peaceful place where Bilbo and his friends can rest before continuing their quest.

THE SHIRE

The home of hobbits, the Shire is a simple land of rolling fields, good food and friendly folk. Bilbo lives here in a hobbit-hole just north of the large city of Hobbiton. It is here that his adventure with Thorin and his companions begins.

EREBOR

The Lonely Mountain – once it was the ancient palace of the Dwarven Kings under the Mountain, but now it is the home of the dragon, Smaug the Terrible. The final destination for Thorin and his companions, the Lonely Mountain's depths contain riches untold and dangers beyond imagination.

HALL OF THE ELVEN KING

Home of Thranduil, the Elven King. This home of the Woodland Elves could well be the end of the line for Bilbo and his companions. Luckily for the Company of Dwarves, Bilbo has a cunning plan and a magic ring that might just save the day...

MIRKWOOD

Once a glorious forest, full of life, Mirkwood is now a place of gloom, decay and evil. With deadly river waters that can send you into a deep sleep and creepy monsters that lurk in the shadows, Mirkwood is not a place for the faint of heart.

THE MISTY MOUNTAINS

A vast mountain range full of danger. Below them are huge caverns filled with Goblins and the terrible abode of the Goblin King – Goblin Town. It is no less dangerous above the ground in the Misty Mountains either. If the raging winds and storms don't sweep you from the path, then a boulder thrown by a Stone Giant just might!

Gandalf

One of the most powerful Wizards in all of Middle-earth, Gandalf is wise and cunning. He has a soft spot for hobbits and sees that Bilbo's many hidden talents and strengths make him the perfect choice to help Thorin Oakenshield on his quest.

There is more to Gandalf than meets the eye. One of the ancient defenders of Middle-earth, it is his purpose to defend the world from evil.

On the way to the Lonely Mountain, Gandalf hears news that an ancient evil is returning to Middle-earth – a terrible enemy that he must try and stop.

The Elves are old friends of Gandalf and even have another name for him: Mithrandir.

When Elrond reads the runes on Gandalf's sword, Glamdring, he tells him that it was once the sword of an ancient and powerful King.

Gandalf is a member of the White Council. Made up of great Wizards and other magical beings, it is an ancient group that forever works to keep evil in check and Middle-earth safe.

A master Wizard, Gandalf is particularly skilled in conjuring and controlling fire in many different forms. From blinding flashes, to flaming explosions, Gandalf proves time and again that his magical powers are a match for any enemy.

Gandalf has visited the Shire many times over the years. He met Bilbo and his mother when Bilbo was a young boy – perhaps even then Gandalf saw hidden strengths in this tiny hobbit?

DID YOU KNOW?

Hobbits know Gandalf as someone who makes particularly amazing fireworks or 'whizz-poppers' for their parties!

BILBO'S BOTTLES

The Dwarves are thirsty! All of these bottles look the same,
but only one is a bottle of Bilbo's finest nettle wine. Can you spot the
bottle which is slightly different? That's the one that contains the wine!

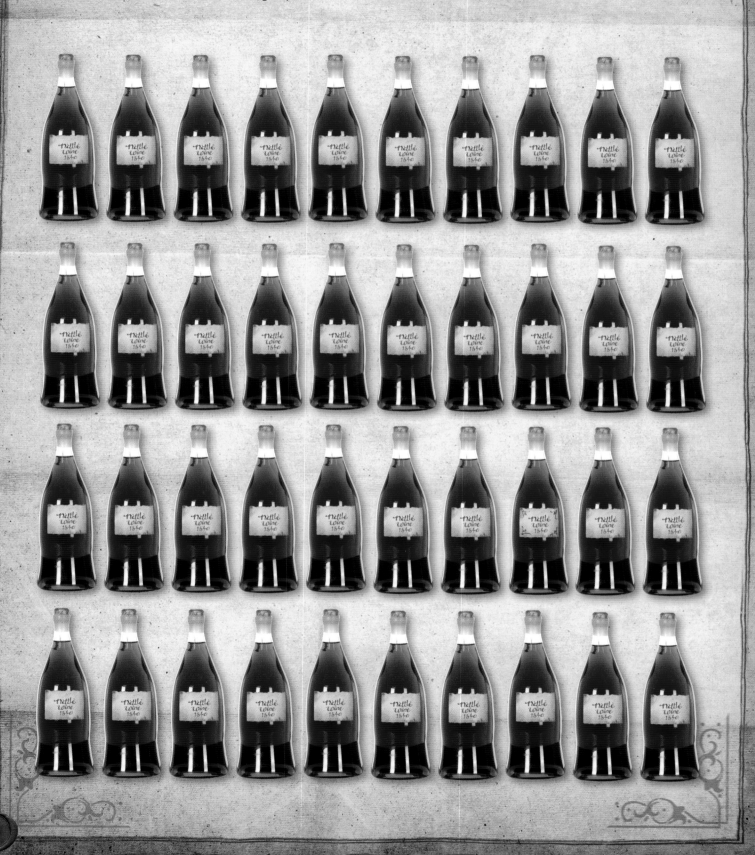

Bilbo Baggins

Thorin Oakenshield

As a young Dwarf Prince, Thorin witnessed the great fire-breathing dragon, Smaug, destroy the Dwarf Kingdom of Erebor. Thorin is now leading a Company of 13 Dwarves (including himself) and one reluctant hobbit to reclaim his ancestors' home and treasure.

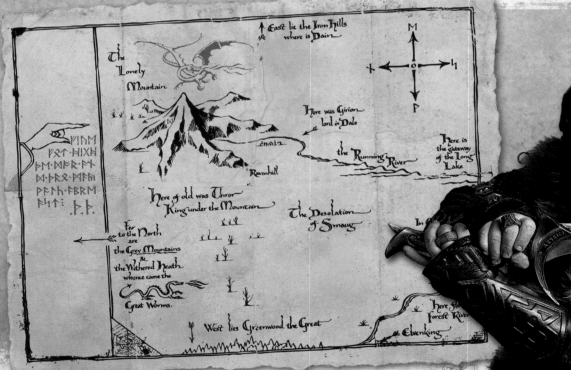

To help in his quest, Gandalf gives Thorin a map and key to the treasure in the Lonely Mountain. Both were made by the ancient Dwarf King, Thror.

Thorin is strong and a fearless fighter, even though he is over 150 years old!

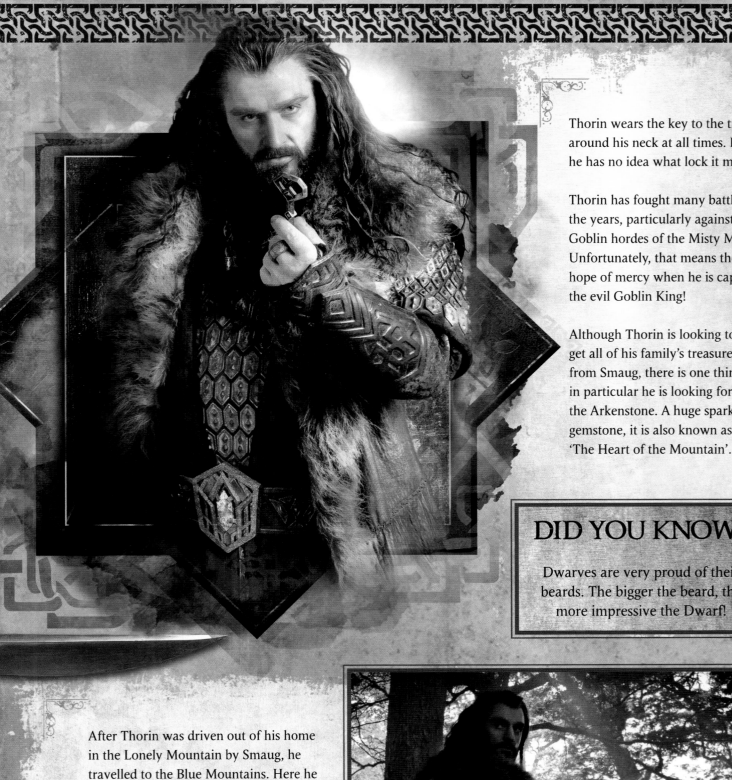

Thorin wears the key to the treasure around his neck at all times. However, he has no idea what lock it might open.

Thorin has fought many battles over the years, particularly against the Goblin hordes of the Misty Mountains. Unfortunately, that means there is little hope of mercy when he is captured by the evil Goblin King!

Although Thorin is looking to get all of his family's treasure back from Smaug, there is one thing in particular he is looking for – the Arkenstone. A huge sparkling gemstone, it is also known as 'The Heart of the Mountain'.

DID YOU KNOW?

Dwarves are very proud of their beards. The bigger the beard, the more impressive the Dwarf!

After Thorin was driven out of his home in the Lonely Mountain by Smaug, he travelled to the Blue Mountains. Here he spent many years as a blacksmith before beginning his quest to restore his family and reclaim his throne.

SACK SEARCH

What a muddle – all of Bilbo's friends have been tied up in sacks by the Trolls.
Help Bilbo make sure he has released them all by finding their names in the grid below.
Names can go left, right, up, down or diagonally!

THORIN   DWALIN   BALIN   FILI   KILI   DORI   NORI

R	B	H	E	E	F	O	M	R	H	N	I	N	L	E	D
L	U	S	N	I	C	I	R	R	D	W	I	M	M	O	W
I	O	B	L	S	W	S	E	C	H	E	N	O	C	H	A
N	I	I	M	O	R	M	T	N	T	U	U	R	A	I	L
G	I	E	R	O	K	B	O	R	W	I	N	I	T	S	I
A	L	L	V	C	B	L	D	R	D	N	H	E	R	I	N
R	C	O	I	M	I	O	O	M	L	O	E	R	T	E	L
H	S	W	I	W	D	E	R	Y	O	T	R	F	T	S	M
Y	G	E	T	N	G	I	D	W	E	O	H	I	E	T	S
L	A	N	I	R	O	H	T	S	A	L	O	H	E	T	F
T	C	F	E	T	M	E	B	A	L	I	N	M	T	S	O
R	U	F	I	B	P	I	I	O	T	T	M	Z	G	R	I
O	Y	O	E	K	P	N	N	I	L	I	K	A	W	A	F
M	S	T	O	E	O	T	E	H	E	O	C	O	R	T	N
I	O	E	C	R	E	S	O	B	Z	O	B	O	F	U	R
S	R	L	I	T	D	V	U	M	E	D	T	S	E	O	C

ORI   OIN   GLOIN   BIFUR   BOFUR   BOMBUR

BOOKMARK BLADES

Keep your place in books with these noble weapons from
the Goblin wars and you will never lose your way in the search for knowledge.

If you don't want to cut your book, trace these designs on to card or photocopy them.

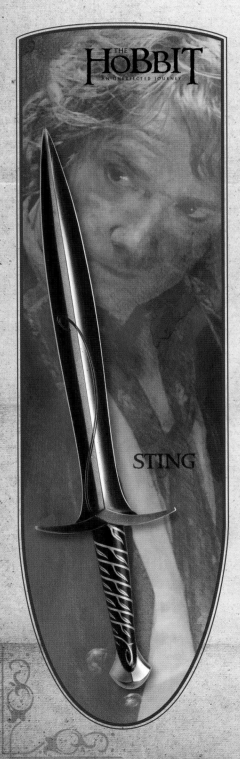

STING

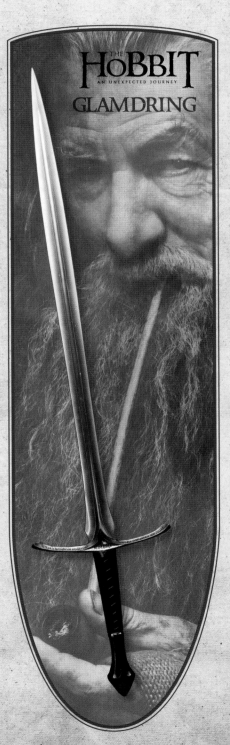

GLAMDRING

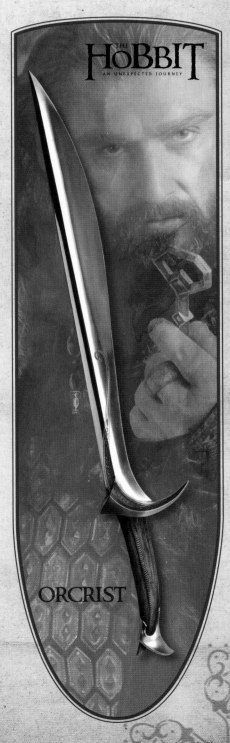

ORCRIST

BOOKMARK BLADES

Keep your place in books with these noble weapons from
the Goblin wars and you will never lose your way in the search for knowledge.

DID YOU KNOW?

Thorin's sword, Orcrist, is known as Biter to Goblins.

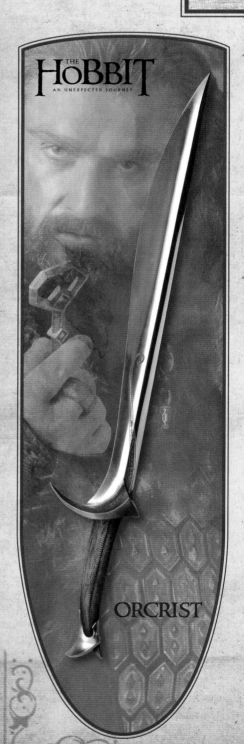

ORCRIST

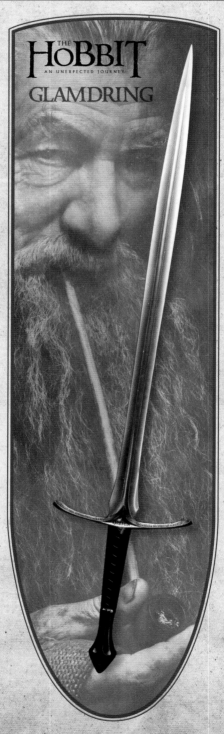

GLAMDRING

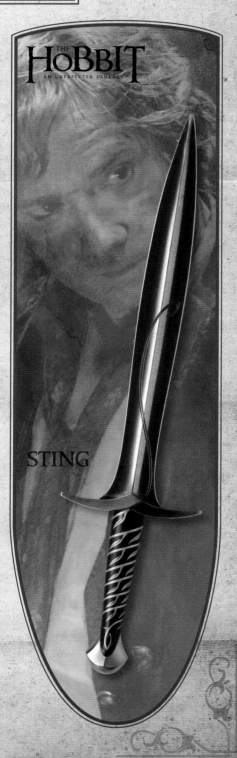

STING

MOON RUNES

Show your wisdom and use the key to help
Elrond read the hidden message on Thorin's map.

A	B	C	D	E	F	G	H	I	J	K	L	M
ᚠ	ᛒ	ᛁ	ᛚ	ᛗ	ᛘ	ᚣ	ᚼ	ᚾ	ᛁ	ᛂ	ᛁ	ᛏ

N	O	P	Q	R	S	T	U	V	W	X	Y	Z

STAND BY THE GREY

STONE WHEN THE THRUSH

KNOCKS AND THE SETTING

SUN WITH THE LAST LIGHT

OF DURINS DAY WILL SHINE

UPON THE KEYHOLE.

East lie the Iron Hills
where is Dain

THE COMPANY OF DWARVES

FILI THE DWARF

A noble Dwarf from the royal line of Durin. Raised by his uncle, Thorin, Fili is one of the youngest Dwarves in the Company. While he is a skilled fighter, Fili has never travelled far in the world and has little idea of the challenges ahead. Indeed, Fili has spent most of his life in the Blue Mountains and has never even seen the far off mountain of Erebor! However, the chance to claim part of its riches and have his name written into legend is more than enough reason to make him join the quest.

KILI THE DWARF

Fili's younger brother, Kili, usually acts before he thinks. Courageous and brave, Kili aims to make a name for himself within the Company and prove his worth. Trained with weapons from an early age, Kili is an expert with a bow.

Filled with the confidence of youth, Kili is certain of his abilities and faces every danger without fear. It's lucky that he is actually as skilled with weapons as he believes, or he would find himself in serious trouble.

BALIN THE DWARF

One of the oldest Dwarves in the group, Balin is a Dwarf Lord. He has led a life filled with many battles, yet he is wise and gentle at heart. One of Thorin's closest friends and advisors, Balin is always ready to offer his opinion and help.

While he would never let his close friend, Thorin, know, Balin has secret doubts about the quest. Uncertain of the wisdom of even starting out on such a dangerous path, Balin is not sure any of them will return alive.

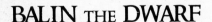

DWALIN THE DWARF

Dwalin is never afraid to say what is on his mind, no matter what people might think. A famous warrior, he is proud and brave. Always loyal, he firmly believes that Thorin's quest will be successful and see the return of the Kings under the Mountain. Most Dwarves don't like Elves, but Dwalin *really* doesn't like them! In fact Dwalin doesn't really like anyone who isn't a Dwarf. To earn his trust and respect is a hard task for anyone to achieve.

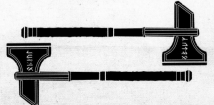

PICTURE PIECES

Which are the correct pieces to complete the picture
of Gandalf, Bilbo and the Company of Dwarves?
Draw a line to place each piece in the correct space.

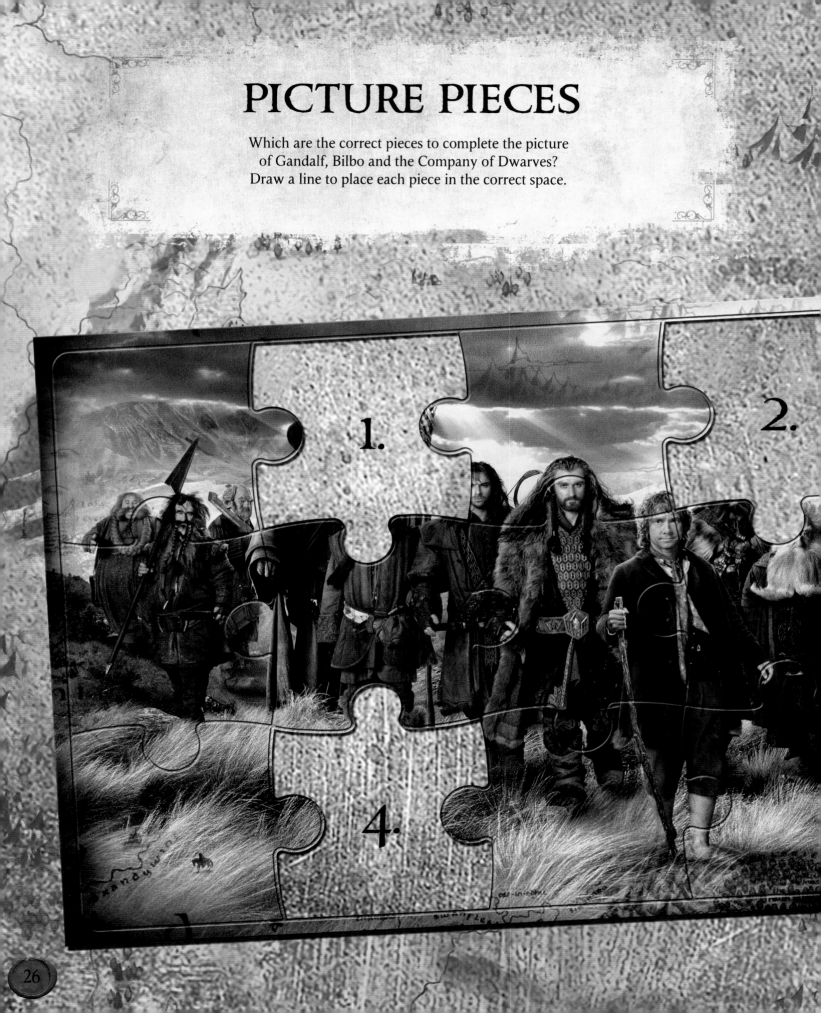

A.

B.

C.

D.

E.

F.

3.

G.

H.

THE COMPANY OF DWARVES

OIN THE DWARF

A distant relation of Thorin, Oin has spent a large sum of money to pay for Thorin's quest. Brave and clever, Oin is also rather hard of hearing. He is the healer of the group and skilled in making medicines from herbs.

Oin is not one of the Dwarves who were forced out of their home in Erebor, but was born and raised among the Northern Dwarves. Even though the quest is not to help reclaim his own family's throne, nevertheless as a loyal Dwarf, Oin sees it as his duty to help.

GLOIN THE DWARF

Oin's brother, Gloin, has a temper almost as large as his strength and bravery. One of the only Dwarves who is married, he is the father of a young Dwarf named Gimli, who will grow up to have adventures even more legendary than his father's.

His wife also has a beard almost as impressive as Gloin himself! Of all the Dwarves in Thorin's group, Gloin is the most likely to speak his mind or challenge those in charge, no matter the consequences.

BOFUR THE DWARF

Bofur's love of good food, fun and music means he has more in common with hobbits than other Dwarves. Always willing to see the best in whatever life brings his way, he often blurts out things without thinking.

Bofur is not as brave as some other Dwarves, but he'll do his best to help defend his friends if they are in danger. Instantly likeable, Bofur is the heart and soul of the party, always willing to cheer up his fellow travellers with a song.

BOMBUR THE DWARF

Bofur's brother and Bifur's cousin, Bombur is the chief cook in the Company. With an appetite as large as his waistline, Bombur spends a lot of time wondering where the next meal is coming from!

Despite his large size (which often gets him into some amusing scrapes), Bombur is quite a fighter. You certainly wouldn't want to get between him and his dinner anyway, that's for sure!

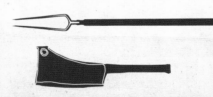

A HELPING HAND

Have you got the wisdom to be a master potion maker like Oin?
Use your number skills to solve these puzzles and prove yourself.

PUZZLE 1

Each of these runes stands for one of the numbers 1, 2, 3, or 4. Can you match the runes to the correct numbers and solve the puzzles?

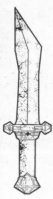

The first sum is:

```
    A  B  C
 +  C  A  A
 ─────────
 =  B  D  B
```

The second sum is:

```
    D  B  B
 −  B  A  C
 ─────────
 =  A  C  A
```

A = ☐   B= ☐   C= ☐   D= ☐

PUZZLE 2

Oin has a problem measuring ingredients for an ointment. Can you help?

Oin has two jars. One of them holds exactly 5 litres of water, the other one holds exactly 3 litres. How can Oin measure exactly 4 litres of water with these two jars? You are allowed to pour away some water.

PUZZLE 3

Oin's recipe sheet has been damaged! Look at the number stack and see if you can work out the missing numbers in the recipe.

				38	☐	49			
		11	22	☐	22	11		
	9	12	6	☐	6	12	9	
7	3	5	2	34	2	5	3	7

 ## PUZZLE 4

Look closely at the numbers for ingredients in the circles. The numbers in each circle of ingredients follow a pattern. Look closely and see if you can find the pattern, then complete the final circle.

 ## PUZZLE 5

Nori has a puzzle for you as well. Can you work it out?

If Oin has 5 potions and you take away 2, how many potions do you have?

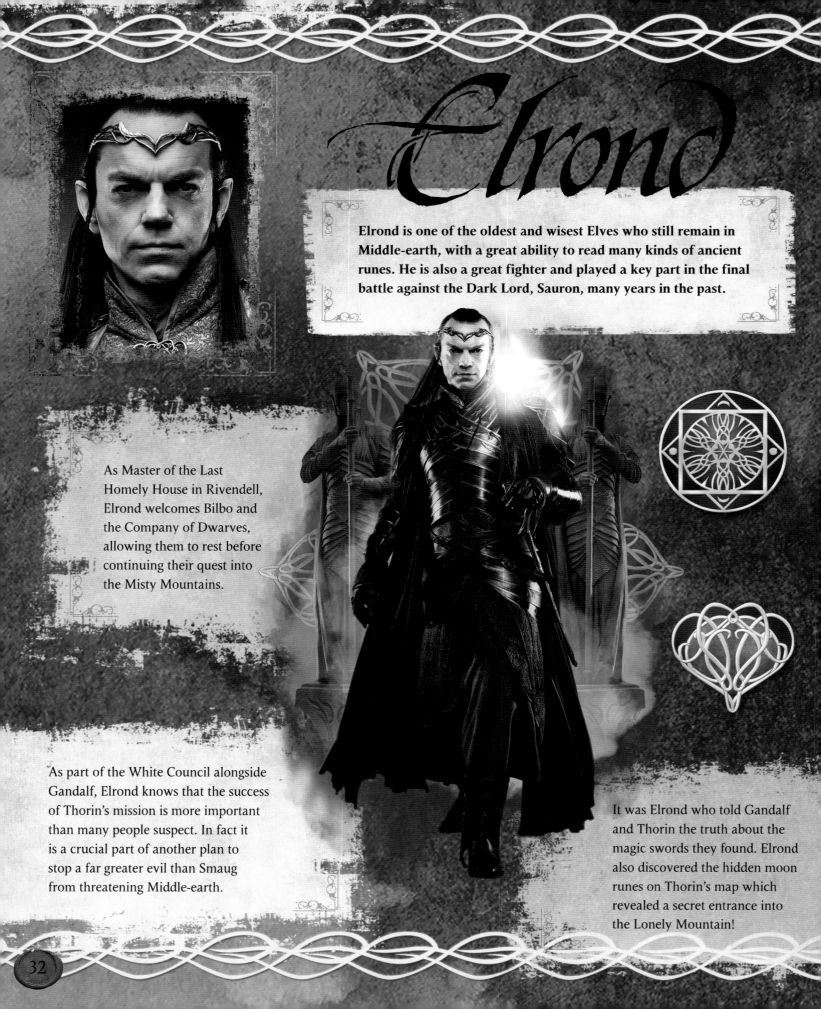

Elrond

Elrond is one of the oldest and wisest Elves who still remain in Middle-earth, with a great ability to read many kinds of ancient runes. He is also a great fighter and played a key part in the final battle against the Dark Lord, Sauron, many years in the past.

As Master of the Last Homely House in Rivendell, Elrond welcomes Bilbo and the Company of Dwarves, allowing them to rest before continuing their quest into the Misty Mountains.

As part of the White Council alongside Gandalf, Elrond knows that the success of Thorin's mission is more important than many people suspect. In fact it is a crucial part of another plan to stop a far greater evil than Smaug from threatening Middle-earth.

It was Elrond who told Gandalf and Thorin the truth about the magic swords they found. Elrond also discovered the hidden moon runes on Thorin's map which revealed a secret entrance into the Lonely Mountain!

MAGIC SQUARES

Can you help Gandalf solve Elrond's tricky number puzzle?
Fill in all the empty squares so that every row, column and small
3x3 square contains all the numbers from 1 to 9.

THE COMPANY OF DWARVES

DORI THE DWARF

Dori is the strongest of all the Dwarves and the elder brother of Nori and Ori. Dori never looks on the bright side of things and always thinks the worst is going to happen. He really cares about his brothers and spends most of his time looking out for Ori.

Dori and his brothers are distant relatives of Thorin. He might not always believe that the Company will succeed in their quest, but Dori would never give less than 100% effort to get the job done.

NORI THE DWARF

A Dwarf who spends most of his time in trouble, Nori is always up to something – and that something is usually illegal. An expert at picking locks, if something dubious needs doing, Nori is your Dwarf.

It is rumoured that the only reason Nori joined the quest in the first place is because he was on the run from trouble in his own town and needed to get away fast! He doesn't always get along with his brothers, but Nori will protect them until his dying breath.

ORI THE DWARF

The youngest of the three brothers, Ori is a brilliant artist. Like Bilbo, Ori keeps a journal and spends a lot of time writing and drawing in it. Most of the time Ori is relatively quiet and polite, but he has a surprising amount of courage and determination. He seems to spend a lot of his time being bossed about by his brothers, but it doesn't mean he won't stand up for himself when the time is right. Ori also happens to be quite a good shot with a catapult!

BIFUR THE DWARF

The first thing anyone notices about Bifur is usually the rusting remains of an Orc axe that is stuck in his head! Unable to talk, Bifur grunts and uses hand signals to communicate.

Unlike most of the others in the Company of Dwarves, Bifur is not directly related to Thorin. He is not of noble lineage, but is descended from miners and smithies.

CHOOSE YOUR WEAPON

The path to the Lonely Mountain is difficult, dangerous and deadly to those who are unarmed. Use these pictures to help design your own legendary weapon to wield in battle.

Dwarven weapons have sharp corners and angles on their blades and handles.

Like Orcrist, weapons designed by Elves are smoothly curved and elegant.

Why not use the runes on page 23 to write something on your weapon?

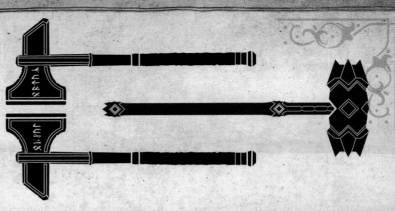

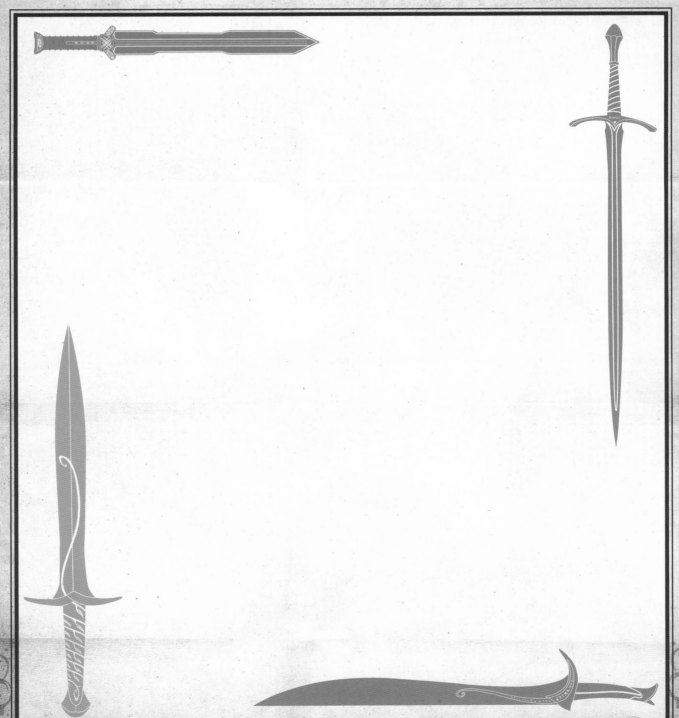

MEET YOUR MATCH

Answer the questions and follow the paths to find out which member of the Company you are most like. Start at the top, give your answers and follow the arrows to reveal your Company alter ego.

I'm quite old.

Would you say that you are wise?

Yes, I'm as wise as an owl.

Not really, no.

Do your friends do what you suggest?

Which weapon would you choose: sword or hammer?

Yes, all the time.

Often they listen to someone else.

Sword. I prefer a sharp weapon.

Hammer. Me SMASH!

Do you believe in magic?

Does your mouth run away with you? Are you talkative?

Magic is all around us.

I'll believe it when I see it.

No, I try to think before I speak.

Yes, I do blurt things out a bit.

Wise and mysterious, you're as magical as GANDALF.

You'd make a great leader and King. Just like THORIN.

You're forthright and loyal, like DWALIN.

Are you old or young?

I'm pretty young.

Do you love good food?

No, food is just fuel for action.

Of course! When's dinner?

Do you act before you've thought things through?

Do you think you're brave?

Yes, if you don't act nothing gets done!

No. Look before you leap!

Yes, I'm as brave as a lion.

Not really.

Are you known for having a temper?

Would you like to grow an impressive beard?

Do you like making up and writing stories?

No, I'm quite calm.

Temper? Me! GRRRRR!

Yes, the bigger the better!

No, a bit of face fur is enough for me!

No, I prefer singing songs.

Yes, I love writing stories.

Strong and quick to act, you're just like GLOIN.

Full of energy and life, BOFUR is your match.

Just like BILBO, you're a quiet hero in the making.

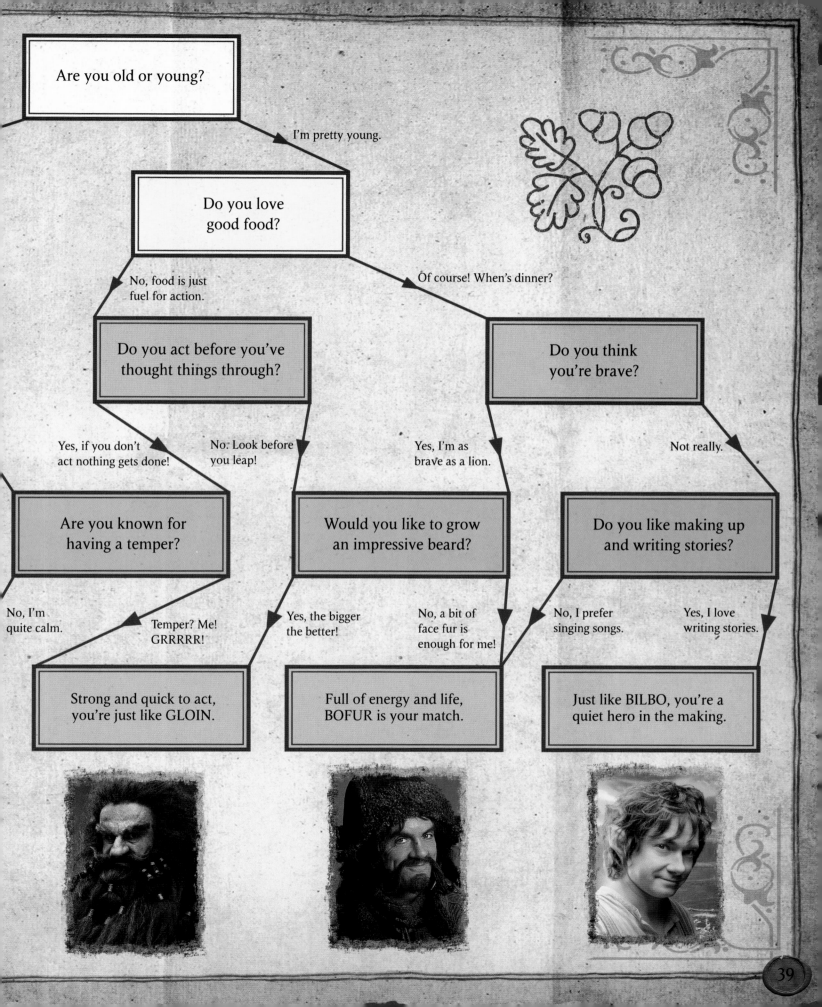

TO ARMS!

Help the Dwarves get ready for battle
by matching them to their weapons.

THORIN

FILI

DWALIN

ORI

BOFUR

BOMBUR

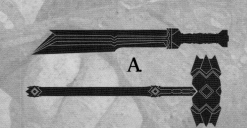

A.

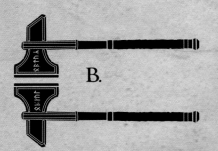

B.

C.

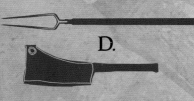

D.

E.

F.

INTO BATTLE!

EYE OF THE BEHOLDER

Middle-earth is a mystical and magical place where things are not
always as they seem, much like the remarkable Bilbo Baggins.

Take a look at these pieces of Middle-earth magic that you can use to amaze your friends.

ILLUSION 1:

Close or cover your RIGHT eye. Now keep looking at the dragonfly on the right.
Slowly move the page towards and away from you and you will suddenly see that
Bilbo has disappeared! Perhaps it's the Ring at work...

ILLUSION 2:

Sometimes what you are looking for can be right there in front of you and you don't even know it.
Stare at the picture for about 30 seconds without blinking. Now look away at a blank white
piece of paper and blink a lot. Whose face has appeared?

ILLUSION 3:
Magic and illusion are powerful tools that can trick even the wisest Wizard. Take a close look at this wine cup. Is it really a wine cup, or a picture of heads, face to face? You decide...

ILLUSION 4:
Your mind can be tricked into seeing what it wants to see. Look closely at the black dot in the middle and you will slowly see the mists begin to clear...

ILLUSION 5:
An enemy cannot harm you if they cannot trust their eyes. Look closely at this image. Are lines a and b parallel? Why not get a ruler and check...

A.

B.

TO THE RESCUE

Goblins have captured Bilbo and the rest of the Company! Show Gandalf the way through the caves and past the guards to the finish so he can free his friends.

START

FINISH

DWARF DOUBLE

There are 10 differences between these pictures of Dori, Kili and Bifur.
Can you spot them all? Circle them on the bottom picture.

A.

B.

Gollum

The Misty Mountains are home to many strange creatures – and none are more strange than Gollum. Pale and shrunken from years of living alone in the dark, Gollum seems quite mad when Bilbo first meets him.

Gollum is not this strange creature's real name. In fact Gollum is actually a hobbit-like creature called Sméagol! He has lived for so many years in the dark caves under the mountains that he doesn't look much like a hobbit any more though!

His 'precious' is an ordinary-looking gold ring and his prized possession. When Gollum thinks that Bilbo has stolen it, he flies into a rage.

DID YOU KNOW?

Gollum loves playing games, especially ones with riddles. In fact he loves games as much as he likes eating fish... or hobbitses.

Gollum lives alone in the middle of a vast underground lake. He knows the caves under the Misty Mountains better than anyone.

He has spent so long on his own that he has started to lose his mind with loneliness. In fact over the years he has become so lonely that he now talks to himself and even his 'precious' ring.

RIDDLES IN THE DARK

When Bilbo stumbles across Gollum in the dark caves under the Misty Mountains he must use his wits in a challenge of riddles. Are you clever enough to take the challenge too? Check your answers on page 61.

RIDDLE 1:

What has roots that nobody sees
Is taller than the trees
Up, up it goes,
And yet never grows?

SOLUTION:

RIDDLE 2:

Voiceless it cries,
Wingless flutters,
Toothless bites,
Mouthless mutters

SOLUTION:

RIDDLE 3:

It cannot be seen, cannot be felt,
Cannot be heard, cannot be smelt.
It lies behind stars and under hills,
And empty holes it fills,
It comes first and follows after,
Ends life, kills laughter.

SOLUTION:

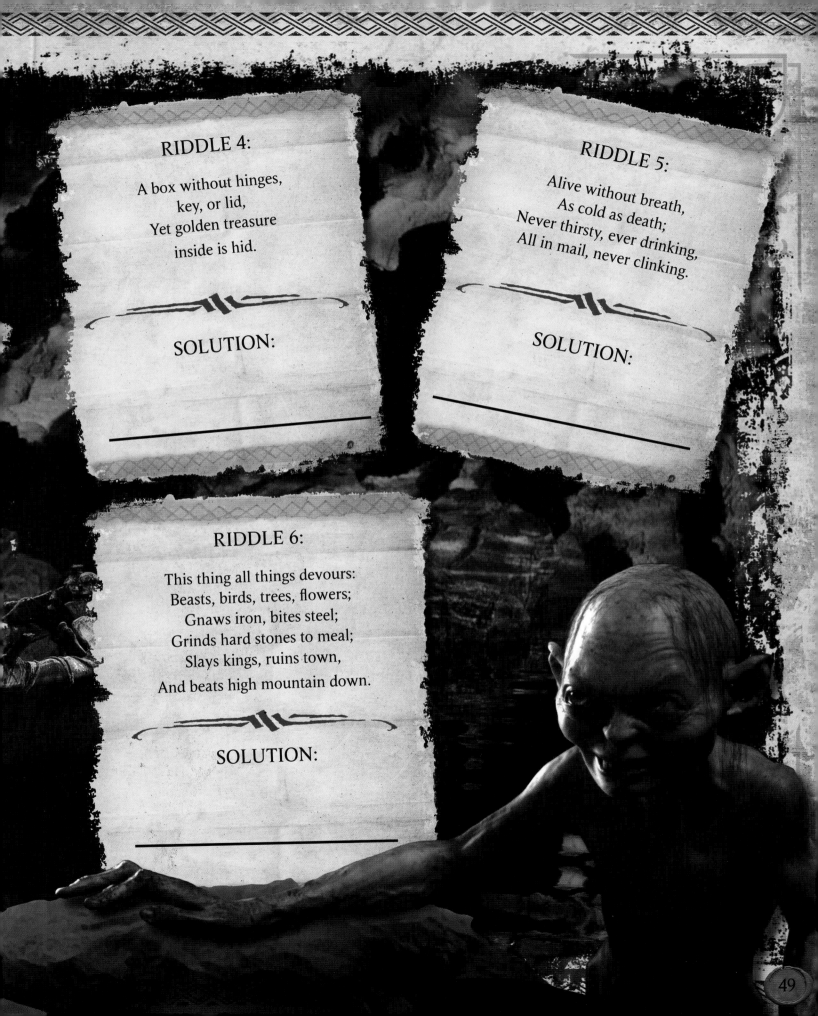

RIDDLE 4:

A box without hinges,
key, or lid,
Yet golden treasure
inside is hid.

SOLUTION:

RIDDLE 5:

Alive without breath,
As cold as death;
Never thirsty, ever drinking,
All in mail, never clinking.

SOLUTION:

RIDDLE 6:

This thing all things devours:
Beasts, birds, trees, flowers;
Gnaws iron, bites steel;
Grinds hard stones to meal;
Slays kings, ruins town,
And beats high mountain down.

SOLUTION:

BILBO'S ESCAPE

Bilbo has stolen Gollum's precious and is trying to escape from the Misty Mountains. Get a counter and a die and see if you can help him find his way out of the caves before Gollum catches up.

1. START

2.

3. Ooops. You stumble in the dark. Fill in 2 extra boxes while you get up.

4.

6.

5.

7. Sting is glowing! Fill in 1 more box while you stop to cover it up so it doesn't give you away.

8.

9.

10.

11.

RULES:

Roll the die and move your counter. Put a cross in a box here every time you roll the die. If you fill them all in before you reach freedom, then Gollum has caught you and you're lunch!

To play again, simply draw your own boxes on a piece of paper.

COUNTDOWN

☐ ☐ ☐ ☐ ☐ ☐
☐ ☐ ☐ ☐ ☐ ☐

15.

Slip on the Ring and disappear! Fill in 1 box and jump to number 17.

16.

17.

19.

20.

FREEDOM! You've escaped Gollum. But there's still a long way to go until you reach the Lonely Mountain!

FINISH

14.

Take a giant leap over Gollum. Fill in 1 box and jump to number 20. **18.**

Bother! Your buttons are stuck on the door. Fill in 1 space while you squeeze out.

13.

12.

Stop to hide from a Goblin patrol. Fill in 2 more boxes.

Gandalf

THE LOST KEY

Alas, the Goblin King has taken Thorin's key to Erebor from him.
Can you select the correct key from the six shadows below?

**THORIN'S KEY
TO EREBOR**

A.

B.

C.

D.

E.

F.

Thranduil

An old and powerful Elf, Thranduil is a cunning warrior who has fought in many battles. As the Elvenking he rules the Wood Elves who live in Mirkwood. He is also the father of an Elf called Legolas who will go on to have his own great adventures with Bilbo's cousin, Frodo.

Like most Elves, Thranduil doesn't really like Dwarves – especially Thorin and his Company. In fact, when he finds Thorin and his friends wandering in Mirkwood, he orders his Wood Elves to take them prisoner.

Thranduil knows how to throw a party and one of his celebrations gives Bilbo the perfect chance to help free his friends and escape from Mirkwood.

Unlike many creatures who pass through Mirkwood, Thranduil and his Wood Elves are not scared of the fearsome monsters that lurk in the shadows. Indeed, if it weren't for Thranduil's people saving them, Thorin and his companions would surely have died deep in the woods.

ON A ROLL

Bilbo has had a cunning plan to help the Company escape. Help him work out which path to roll the barrels along to find a way out of the Halls of the Elven King.

A.   B.   C.

ESCAPE THE WARGS!

A vicious pack of Wargs approach and poor Bilbo has no place to hide!
Be quick and help him find his way to Bofur, who can help him to safety.

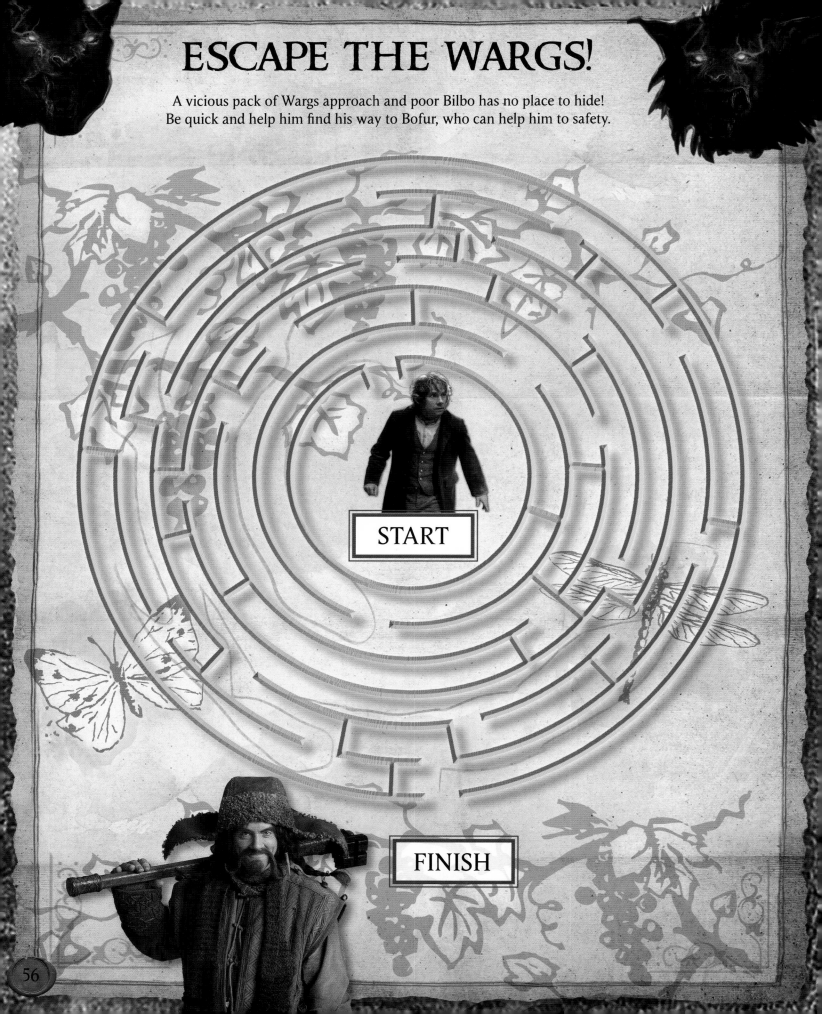

START

FINISH

ORI'S ART

Ori needs a picture of Bilbo for his journal.
Look at the picture on the left and copy it square by square
into the larger grid below to complete the portrait.

AN UNEXPECTED QUIZ

So you think you know all there is to know about Bilbo's adventures?
Then take this quiz to see what you have learned about the Company and their quest.

QUESTION 1:
Where does Bilbo live?

Rivendell, Mirkwood or Bag End.

QUESTION 2:
Which of these was not in the Company of Dwarves?

Oin, Boing, Gloin.

QUESTION 3:
What does Thorin Oakenshield wear around his neck?

Thror's Key, Bilbo's map, Galadriel's necklace.

QUESTION 4:
Which weapon is this?

QUESTION 5:
What is the name of the son of Gloin?

Frodo, Gimli, Ori.

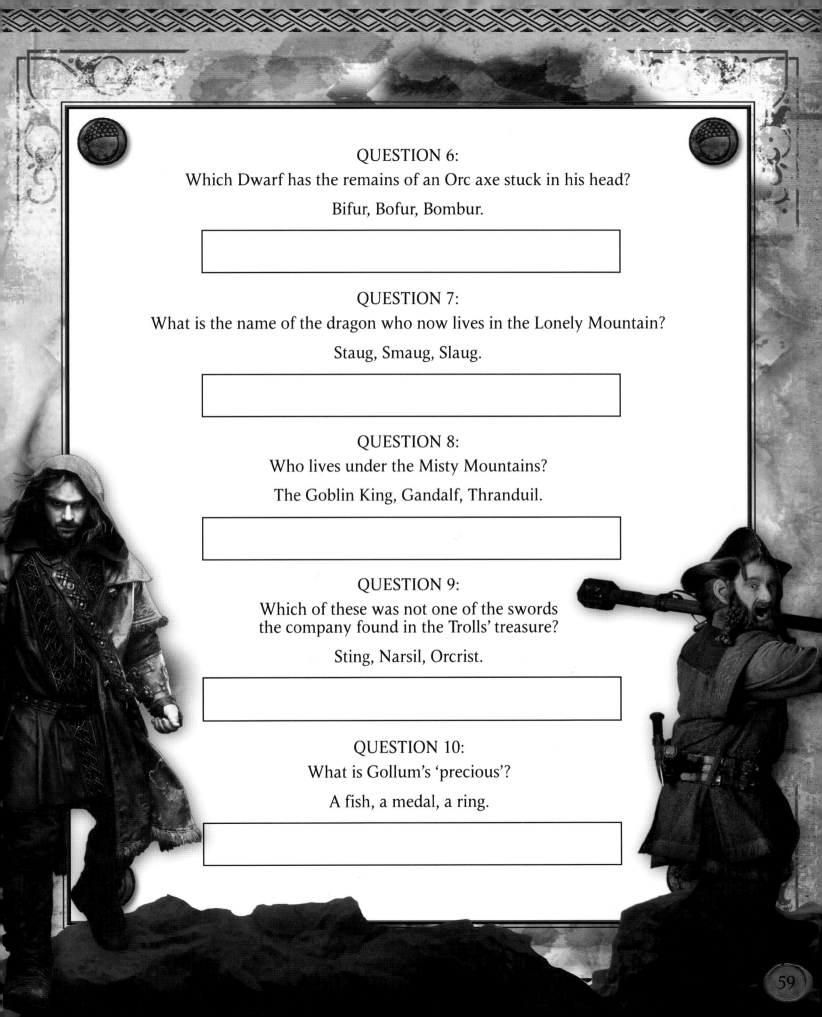

QUESTION 6:

Which Dwarf has the remains of an Orc axe stuck in his head?

Bifur, Bofur, Bombur.

QUESTION 7:

What is the name of the dragon who now lives in the Lonely Mountain?

Staug, Smaug, Slaug.

QUESTION 8:

Who lives under the Misty Mountains?

The Goblin King, Gandalf, Thranduil.

QUESTION 9:

Which of these was not one of the swords
the company found in the Trolls' treasure?

Sting, Narsil, Orcrist.

QUESTION 10:

What is Gollum's 'precious'?

A fish, a medal, a ring.

ANSWERS

PANTRY PUZZLE page 10

BILBO'S BOTTLES page 16

SACK SEARCH page 20

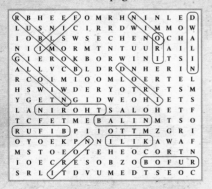

MOON RUNES page 23

Stand by the grey stone when the thrush knocks and the setting sun with the last light of durins day will shine upon the keyhole.

PICTURE PIECES pages 26-27

1=F, 2=B, 3=G, 4=H

A HELPING HAND pages 30-31

PUZZLE 1. A =1, B=3, C=2, D=4

PUZZLE 2. Fill the 5 litre jar completely. Pour the water from the 5 litre jar into the 3 litre jar until it is full. There are 2 litres left in the 5 litre jar. Pour away the water from the 3 litre jar. Then pour the 2 litres from the 5 litre jar into the 3 litre jar. Completely fill the 5 litre jar again. Pour water from the 5 litre jar into the 3 litre jar until it is full. This will only take 1 litre, which will leave 4 litres in the 5 litre jar.

PUZZLE 3.

		38	87	49		
	11	22	66	22	11	
	9	12	6	54	6	12	9
7	3	5	2	34	2	5	3	7

PUZZLE 4. The answer is 35 (the bottom number is the product of multiplying the other 2 numbers together).

PUZZLE 5. The answer is 2 potions. If you take 2, you have 2!

MAGIC SQUARES page 33

4	2	1	5	6	8	9	3	7
7	8	6	2	9	3	4	1	5
9	5	3	4	1	7	2	6	8
5	3	2	8	4	1	7	9	6
6	1	7	9	2	5	8	4	3
8	4	9	3	7	6	5	2	1
3	9	8	1	5	2	6	7	4
2	6	5	7	3	4	1	8	9
1	7	4	6	8	9	3	5	2

TO ARMS! page 40

Thorin = F, Fili = A, Dwalin = B, Ori = C, Bofur = E, Bombur = D.

TO THE RESCUE pages 44-45

DWARF DOUBLE page 46

RIDDLES IN THE DARK pages 48-49

SOLUTION 1: A mountain

SOLUTION 2: The wind

SOLUTION 3: The dark

SOLUTION 4: An egg

SOLUTION 5: A fish

SOLUTION 6: Time

THE LOST KEY page 53

The correct key is D.

ON A ROLL page 55

The right path is C.

ESCAPE THE WARGS! page 56

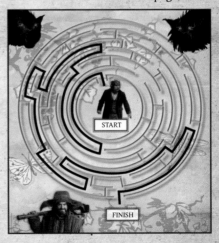

AN UNEXPECTED QUIZ pages 58-59

1. Bag End, 2. Boing, 3. Thror's Key, 4. Glamdring, 5. Gimli, 6. Bifur, 7. Smaug, 8. The Goblin King, 9. Narsil, 10. A ring